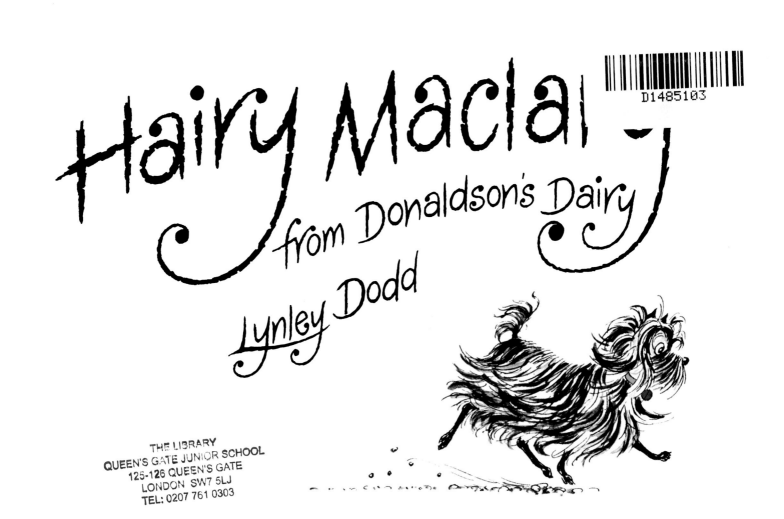

Hairy Maclary

from Donaldson's Dairy

Lynley Dodd

PUFFIN

Out of the gate
and off for a walk
went Hairy Maclary
from Donaldson's Dairy

and Hercules Morse
as big as a horse

with Hairy Maclary
from Donaldson's Dairy.

Bottomley Potts
covered in spots,
Hercules Morse
as big as a horse

and Hairy Maclary
from Donaldson's Dairy.

Muffin McLay
like a bundle of hay,
Bottomley Potts
covered in spots,
Hercules Morse
as big as a horse

and Hairy Maclary
from Donaldson's Dairy.

Bitzer Maloney
all skinny and bony,
Muffin McLay
like a bundle of hay,
Bottomley Potts
covered in spots,
Hercules Morse
as big as a horse

and Hairy Maclary
from Donaldson's Dairy.

Schnitzel von Krumm
with a very low tum,
Bitzer Maloney
all skinny and bony,
Muffin McLay
like a bundle of hay,
Bottomley Potts
covered in spots,
Hercules Morse
as big as a horse

and Hairy Maclary
from Donaldson's Dairy.

With tails in the air
they trotted on down
past the shops and the park
to the far end of town.
They sniffed at the smells
and they snooped at each door,
when suddenly,
out of the shadows
they
saw . . .

SCARFACE CLAW
the toughest Tom
in
town.

"EEEEEOWWWFFTZ!"
said Scarface Claw.

Off with a yowl
a wail and a howl,
a scatter of paws
and a clatter of claws,
went Schnitzel von Krumm
with a very low tum,
Bitzer Maloney
all skinny and bony,
Muffin McLay
like a bundle of hay,
Bottomley Potts
covered in spots,
Hercules Morse
as big as a horse

and Hairy Maclary
from Donaldson's Dairy,

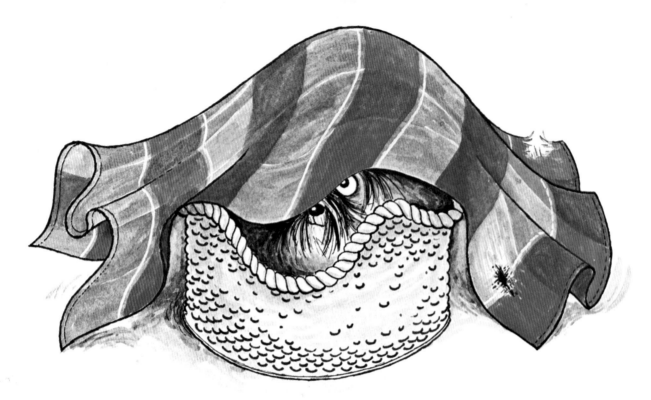

straight back home
to bed.

PUFFIN BOOKS
Published by the Penguin Group: London, New York, Australia, Canada, India, Ireland, New Zealand and South Africa
Penguin Books Ltd, Registered Offices: 80 Strand, London WC2R 0RL, England
puffinbooks.com
First published in New Zealand by Mallinson Rendel Publishers Limited 1983
First published in Great Britain in Puffin Books 1985. Published in this edition 2005, reissued 2008
3 5 7 9 10 8 6 4